For my boys—
Jackson, Tucker, and Walker,
who LOVE trucks

Published by Two Lions, New York | www.apub.com
Amazon, the Amazon logo, and Two Lions are trademarks of
Amazon.com, Inc., or its affiliates.

ISBN-13: 9781542092685 · ISBN-10: 154209268X

The illustrations were created digitally.
Book design by Abby Dening
Printed in China · First Edition · 10 9 8 7 6 5 4 3 2 1

two lions

Scooper and Dumper

LINDSAY WARD

TOWN
SALT YARD

Cold winds blow—
winter's here.
Scooper 'n' Dumper
in first gear!

The best of friends,
working together,
take care of their town
in any weather.

Scooper's teeth
dig with might.
Rock salt mound,
feel the bite!

BEEP!
BEEP!

Bright-blue salt
packs Dumper's bed.
Town is quiet . . .

. . . time to spread!

**Clear the road.
Salt the street.**

Work together,
can't be beat!

A big front loader
too slow for roads.
Scooper stays put
lifting loads.

Sky turns gray.
Snow falls fast,
filling the town
with winter's blast.

Clear the road.
Salt the street.

Work together,
can't be beat!

"Careful, Dumper!
This storm is strong.
Come back quick!
Don't take too long."

"No storm stands
a chance with me.
Don't worry, Scooper.
Just wait, you'll see."

Bright, big city
up ahead.
Spinner ready . . .

. . . time to spread!

Traffic's moving—
the road's all clear.
Lines of cars
give a cheer!

HONK!
HONK!
HONK!
HONK!
BEEP!
HONK!
HONK!
BEEP!
BEEP!
BEEP!
BEEP!
HONK!
BEEP!

"No trouble at all
for a dumper like me.
Happy to help
you cars get free."

DUMPER

Yard's blocked in,
high and thick.
Scooper's digging.
Quick, quick, quick.

Snow drifts.
Hard to steer!
Dumper's wheels
start to veer.

Uh-oh, look out!
Up ahead.

Trucks piled up,
off their tread!

Icy roads.
Slip and slide!
Dumper spins out . . .

. . . off the side!

"Oh no! Help!"
His tires screech.
Wedged in snow—
he's out of reach!

Scooper starts to hesitate. "Dumper's never been this late."

Come in, Flatbed—
I need a lift!
I'm worried Dumper's caught in a drift.

Can Scooper do it?
Leave the yard?
She's not so sure . . .
it could be hard.

"My wheels are big,
and I'm too slow.
Out on the road
I cannot go."

But Dumper's in trouble!
What if he broke down?
Or got lost in the snow
outside of town?

Back on the road
it's getting late.
Trucks piled up,
all left to wait.

Out of gas,
vision's low.
Dumper shivers.
"What's that glow?"

Clear the road.
Salt the street.

Work together,
can't be beat!

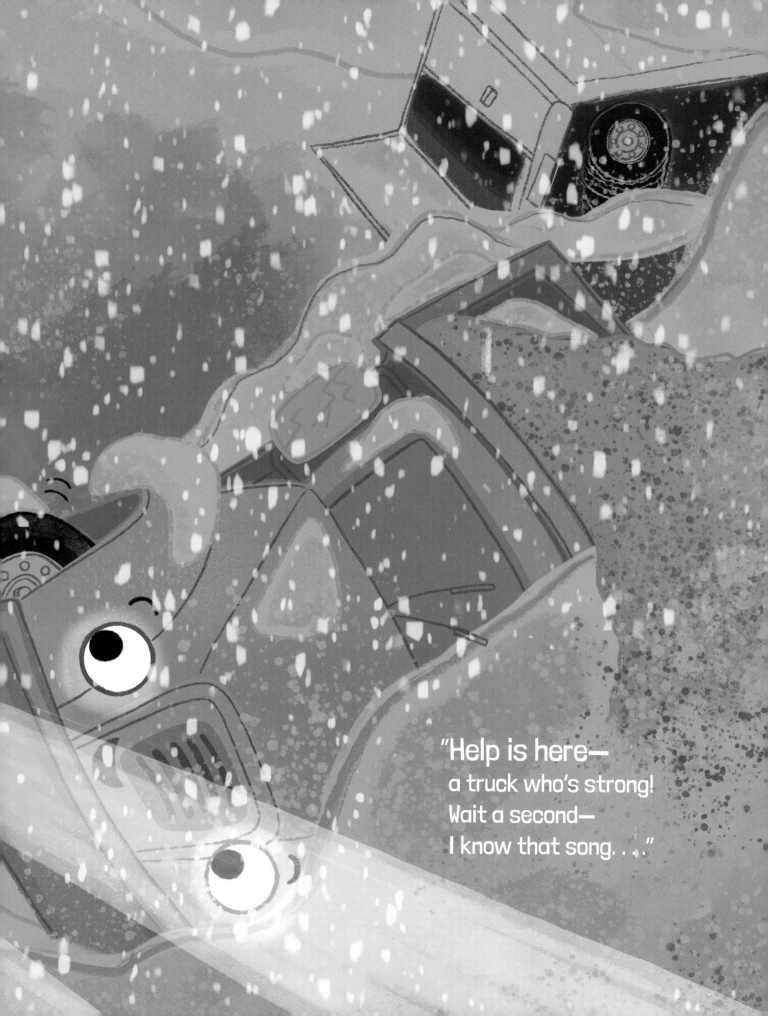

"Help is here—
a truck who's strong!
Wait a second—
I know that song. . . ."

"Scooper's here
to save the day!"
Her yellow bucket
digs away.

Clear the road.
Salt the street.

Work together,
can't be beat!

Scooper 'n' Dumper
comin' through.
No storm too strong.
No ice too blue.

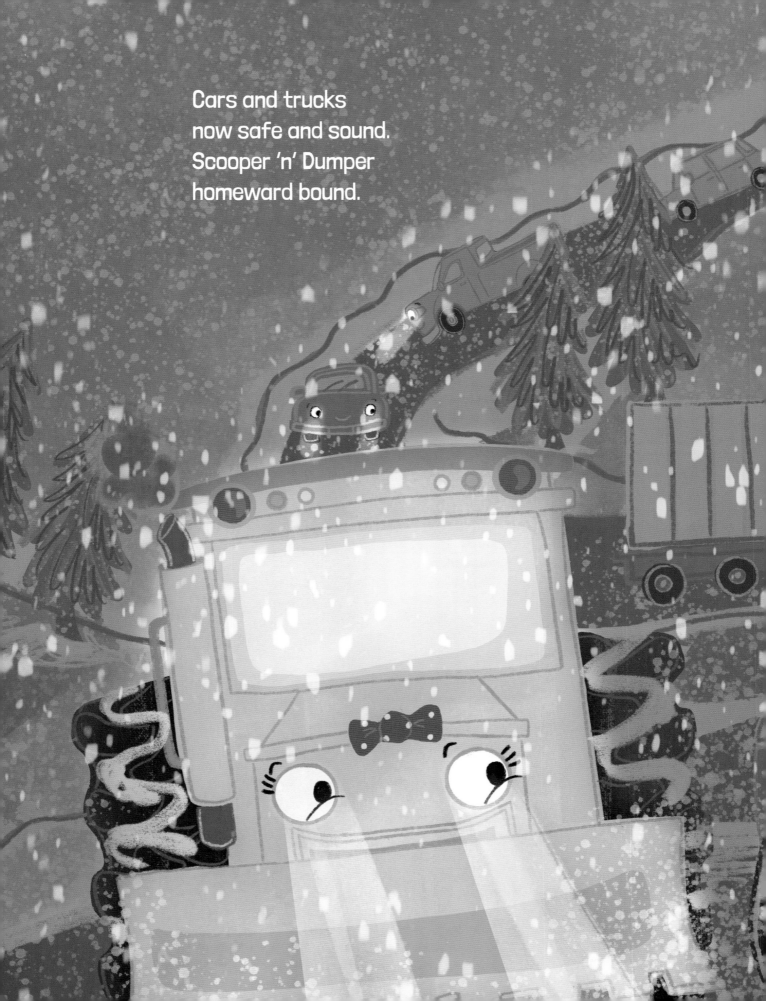

Cars and trucks
now safe and sound.
Scooper 'n' Dumper
homeward bound.